BEWARE OF THE WRATH OF MEDEIA

By Katherine B. Parilli

Print: 978-1-947238-52-7

DeGrawPublishing@comcast.net

De Graw Publishing

Lady Lake, Florida

DEDICATION

This book is dedicated to my parents. Thank you for being there in the rough times as well as the good. Words cannot express my gratitude for the sacrifices that you have made to take care of me in my ongoing health battle. I know that it has been both a financial and emotional strain, yet as hard as things got, you always did your best to make it clear that it was a sacrifice of love.

If that were not enough, when I decided that I wanted to try my hand at publishing my poems and stories, you gladly gave me your support. You have done all in your power to help me make a success of my dreams, and for that I shall forever be grateful.

Thank you for being super parents who never let me get away with giving less than my best, and teaching me that love for God, family, and self means always striving to be the best me that I can possibly be.

BEWARE OF THE WRATH OF MEDEIA

Hi, my name is Medeia Robertson. Of course, you have probably heard about me on the news or read about me in the newspaper. Funny, a man can still be considered a poor unfortunate victim after walking out with all of his wife's hard-earned money to give it to some surgically enhanced Barbie doll, kidnap her children, and steal her good name and that barely raises an eyebrow. Let the bruised woman get even with the thieving, cheating scoundrel and suddenly her name is bound with all that is evil. Now where is the justice in that I ask you? Of course, how would you know? You are but a stranger doomed to suffer behind these same four torturous walls as I.

I know that as hated as I am on the outside, it is even worse for me here, locked up among those they dare to call my peers. My peers, how can you be my peer? Have you determinedly climbed the perilous height of mount Everest and looked down upon the fearful world as a conqueror? Have you been cruelly betrayed on every front by the one you have protected and sacrificed for at every turn? I do not think so! Yet my persecutors have taken such delight in comparing me to the rest of this dreamless lot that only sought to serve self.

From that smile on your face I know that you already have some opinion of my guilt, but you are not as certain as the rest. Before you totally side with those who call for my immediate demise, I beg you to hear me out.

Oh, at last maybe I have met one soul who is willing to hear my story before condemning my broken heart to death. It will not take very long; the emotions that landed me here are no different than those of other woman still free to walk beyond these imprisoning walls. Put anyone of those self-absorbed souls in my shoes and you will see that none of them would hesitate to act as I have. Why they would be the first to come to me for advice, and beg for mercy at the feet they have so recently condemned as death incarnate.

Growing up I never imagined that I would be brought so low. I was of royal blood. During the days of Hawaii's lost glory my family were leaders of men, counselors, judges, and known for their ability to locate and combine the healing herbs the land had provided. Years after Hawaii became a state my parents were still sought for their wise counsel. It was at my grandmother's feet that I learned the dying art of combing leaves, herbs, and other special ingredients to form powerful creams and teas that could make the sick well and the well sick.

It is no wonder that with this knowledge I did well in chemistry. My knowledge of chemistry eventually earned me a scholarship to a rather presumptuous private University near Washington D.C. that catered to the sons and daughters of the elite. O how I hated that school! As children of modern privilege, they had no use for an ex-royal. For three years I talked to no one unless I had to, especially my roommate. What a roommate, a skinny girl who used her pom-poms for brains. She hated me and I despised her. She was angered that she had been forced to room with someone whose bloodlines were so passé. The only purpose I could have served her would have been to do her homework, if she had to do any that is. Pretty girls don't need to do homework she would vainly insist. "I do not have to learn anything because I am rich and beautiful. If I wanted to catch an eligible bachelor, like the star football player, all I would have to do is wait until the right moment and bat my little blue eyes and he would be helplessly mine. While you need all those stale books of yours if you want to survive. Your only hope of landing a date would be to glue all those filthy books together and pretend they were alive!" UGH I hated her with all my might, that little Miss Snobby U.

Then one day in the beginning of my junior year two of my professors pulled me aside with a life or death favor. It seemed that the star football player was having some scholastic distress and they were hoping that I might tutor him before he was permanently benched. They were huge football fans, and since one of them was my favorite chemistry teacher I reluctantly agreed.

Trembling slightly, I went to the library to meet my detestable roommate's future date. As I figured, he was as irritating as I had imagined. Things were moving painfully along until he mentioned that he had to do a paper on Medea. This perked my attention since my mother had named me Medeia because she hoped that someday I would become a leader of people as the name implied. So almost by birthright I developed a fascination for the assorted sundry of doomed characters that suffered in that famous Greek tragedy, never dreaming it was to become my death cry.

The idea of helping this repulsive football player in distress who just happened to be named Jason struck my fancy as life imitating art as Medeia once more found herself compelled by outside forces to come to the rescue of a less than agreeable Jason in distress. At first it was an overwhelming task trying to deal with the injured pride of our modern war hero having to be taught by this upstart ex-royal. But then, almost imperceptibly at first, study time became more and more enjoyable as we sat in the back of the rather icy library. Soon we were meeting at lunchtime, walking to classes together, and were totally inseparable. Oh how that tawny airhead croaked and cawed in guttural despair when she saw us walking arm in arm around campus.

Soon after graduation we were married and moved into a small dingy flat; the only thing we could afford after Jason's parents cut him off without a cent as punishment for not marrying the high society girl, they had always hoped he would marry. Since Jason's chosen major had been political science we decided to stay in the D.C area where he could have a chance at landing a good government job. But when time sped by without an offer, he was forced to take a barely livable job as a manager of a small investment company. I was now a desperate mother of two small boys hoping to find a way to pay the rent and buy some food. We were desperate because one of the boys needed to have a tonsillectomy and the company Jason worked offered no health benefits. Then it dawned on me, I remembered a special mixture that my grandmother had taught me years ago that not only helped to sooth dry skin but also diminished wrinkles. It would not cost much to make and with my knowledge of chemistry I was sure that it would not only work, but that it would be a financial success.

Within a year of starting our own business we had moved out of that wretched two-bedroom apartment into a lovely home in a picturesque neighborhood filled with diplomats, politicians, and other Washington elite. Our new home had eight bedrooms, four bathrooms, a powder room, a kitchen the size of a train station, and was overflowing with modern conveniences. Our closest neighbor and dearest friend was a secretary to the President. We hosted picnics attended by capital workers, politicians, and even a few foreign diplomats. We were an overnight success. The toast of D.C. as the politician's wives reveled in their youthful looks and the men their dramatic savings.

All was well, or so I thought. I had no clue of what cruel irony was waiting for me. It was the morning of my tenth wedding anniversary of all dates February 14, 2025. I had dropped the kids off at school as usual and went to pick up Jason's gift, a new shiny red corvette. He would be so delighted when I presented it to him at the office. It was on the way to deliver my special anniversary surprise that I began the most agonizing irony of my humbled life. Why had my mother named me Medeia? Why had I been so fascinated with the misfortunate characters in that horrific Greek tragedy?

There it was in gruesome life size boldness before my panic stung eyes. On a sign advertising my beauty products was the gleaming face of pom-poms for a brain Miss Snobby U herself. Only now her youthful figure came directly from the hands of an expensive plastic surgeon. There was nothing real about her except that infuriating air that said I am better than you Medeia Robertson because I am a modern royal. I was furious to say the least, and was ready to tear into Jason for daring to hire that awful creature to advertise my creams and gels.

Oh, was I in for a shock! As my car door slammed shut, I caught sight of them out of the corner of my eyes walking arm and arm in the parking lot my family's ancient formula had paid for. What a sickening sight it was to see those two acting like school children for the whole world to see.

After they left, I slipped into the office to talk with Bob the head of finances. My world, which I already thought to be at rock bottom, crashed and burned just as Medea's had when her Jason suddenly married Creon's daughter. Every cent of the company was gone. It had been sold out from under me to a foreign investor and placed in that thieving Jason's greedy pocket. The company was gone, my invention stolen. Bob was clueless to my dismay showing me a copy of my signature turning my patent over to the new boss and on the bill of sale. My hurt was turned to anger and I feared there was more folly to be unburied.

I rushed breathlessly to the bank fearing the worse while praying that this was all just a dream. A fearful nightmare due to a forgotten late-night snack and in the morning, all would be well once more. Of course, I was cheerfully reassured that my personal account worth nearly five million had been transferred to a Swiss bank account just as I had ordered two months ago. Two months ago…? When two months ago…? Two months ago, I was out of town burring my mother who had died of a heart attack. How could I have ordered it two months ago? The man just shrugged his fat shoulders and smiled as he said that my husband brought them some papers signed by the both of us ordering the transfer and he had complied. He did not even break into a sweat when I asked him why I would not have come in person to deal with such a huge amount when in the past I would argue over five missing dollars? Nor did he second-guess his negligent actions when the paper he showed me was proven to be an easily identifiable forgery that even a five-year old child could catch.

Well I was stunned and foaming by then. How dare he! How dare they! How dare everyone! What should I do first, shoot him and claw her, claw her and then shoot him? No, I should teach that easily broken porcelain doll a lesson and then shoot him, or…well there was no time for that right now. It was time to pick the children, our children, from school and take them home where I would try to shield them from the ghastly truth about their father for as long as possible.

But they were not at school. They had been picked up earlier in the day by their father and a fabulous looking woman. They told the school that I was very ill and needed to see the children. Now it was becoming clear. First the sign, then the business, all my money, and now my children. She was stealing everything, that wretched little pom-pom from Snobby U. Well she would not get away with it if I could help it.

Like a bloodhound I tracked them down for a year. Searching for my children, searching for the thieves that stole my life and now were trying to steal the very soul of my heart. I loved those children. Now that Jason the snail, the snail like the play I had loved so much, had stolen my life away, they were all that I had left. I did not care about the money. The money was worthless without my children. I realized now that it had all been a plan. The declaration of love, the marriage, all those long years he had claimed to love me had all been a cruel scheme to steal my heart and money. O let me tell you I had worked myself into a frenzy. My imagination had gone into overdrive and all common sense was gone. But there was one thing they had forgotten about, and in this I took comfort, and that was to beware of the wrath of Medeia!

Soon after the fateful anniversary day they were married and dashed off for an around the world honeymoon cruise. It seems Jason's expensive lawyers found a loophole in our marriage license and we were no longer legally married. Shows you what four hundred and seventy-five million can do for a man. I must say that he was not dumb about selling the company for a profit, or about the timing. A week after he sold the company, another unexplainable loophole appeared, this time in my patent rights. It was immediately brought to the new owner's attention and he went out of business a month later. He angrily blamed me insisting that I had conspired to defraud him of millions and he threatened to have me thrown in jail if I did not return him his money.

This made me even more determined to hunt my prey down like a bloodhound on the scent of a sniveling rat. Finally, a clue, a lucky break as the rat came home to roost. He and his plastic bride were going to attend the swearing in of a new senator, that barbarian's father! And all this made possible by my money!

I knew I had to do something. I was certain they would never have come back to U.S. soil if they knew that I was still free to hunt them down. They must have figured that I was rotting in some jail thanks to that anonymous tip that not only ripped apart my patent, but accused the former owner, me of course, of skipping some important safety steps in order to secure greater profits. But red tape was only becoming stronger with the advent of technology and thanks to the wonders of a few well-timed keystrokes files could easily be misplace or deleted leaving me a free woman. Free to hunt down my persecutors and rescue my children.

What should I do I anxiously fretted? There was little time to put into action the elaborate plans I had conceived during the long nights that my eyes overflowed like a rain-soaked dam. Then it came to me, just like Medea; this Medeia had some knowledge of chemicals, brews, and tinctures that could bring down her enemies. And as her enemies had underestimated the first Medea, so had I been lucky enough to be underestimated by mine. It would be a twist of sheer genius right out of the Greek tragedy I once loved. I still had the shiny red corvette I once planned to give my beloved Jason. And now I would give it to him. Oh, not I, for that would be to obvious, but with the aid of a trusted old friend whose wife had left him for another man and who shared my thirst for revenge. He would bring me the herbs I needed to make my special brew that would melt the plastic doll right down to her slimy rotten core. How would this Jason love his surgically crafted bride now as her skin grew dry and blotchy, her lovely hair fell from its precious roots, and her carefully sculpted waist swelled overnight.

Almost lovingly I made the special ancestral brew of revenge. This was not a common Hawaiian brew, but had been painstakingly created by a jilted great-great-great grandmother who spent years seeking the tools of revenge she finally found in a very rare plant. It was a carefully guarded secret, and was the nameless potion that gave my family its name for being wise in the art of herbs both good and bad. My mother had given it to me as a gift on my wedding day, admonishing me to guard it with my life and to use it only in an extreme emergency. Now I added to this family treasure my knowledge of chemistry to make it a much longer lasting lotion that I could apply to the seat where I was positive the preening proud princes would most desire to sit and be admired by her imaginary crowd.

Under an assumed identity in a town mile away I rented a car while my old friend gladly presented my gift as a present from an anonymous admirer. For a week I waited outside their rented home not far from our first two-bedroom apartment. I watched as each afternoon they went for a drive unaware that each day, little by little, some of my special secret seeped into her veins. Already her hair was growing thinner and her once haughty blue eyes looked much older. Her mood at first had been upbeat and cheerful as she wore her tight fitted jeans and low-class blouses to enhance her pleasure while racing down the street in my slick Trojan horse. In all that time the children were never present, the pride of my nemesis too great to be seen with children.

All I can remember about that final dreadful day was that it was a Sunday afternoon. The princes was no longer as pretentious looking as the day that she glared laughingly down from that billboard. Now she wore a hat to cover her baldness, her dress was loose and long to cover her swelling body, and her red blotchy hands were safely tucked under a pair of unfashionably soft cotton gloves. The children carried a picnic basket as they headed to the car. I was relieved that they sat safely in the back seat. I watched awe struck to see just how much they had grown in a year. I longed to run to them, but dared not reveal myself unless the opportune time arose. I followed them from a safe distance and watched as the children ran and played while miss perfect sat brooding under a tree viewing the world from behind a pair of rather darkly tinted sunglasses. Each time the children called to her she pouted and ignored their pleas to join their fun. Jason just dozed under the shade of a tree ignorant of their need to be fussed over. Once or twice they eagerly grabbed at the hands of that slowly melting former beauty queen, but quit when she snapped at their innocent request. Barking the most cutting demands to leave her alone and let her rest caused my heart to rage. How dare she use such words with my children! If she did not want them around why did she steal them from me?

It was all I could do not to race out and slap her disgraceful blue blood mouth. At last I was relieved to see them head towards the car. At least the suffering of my babies was over for now. But to my horror I watched as one of the boys, reluctant to get in the car because he had lost a toy, was rudely grabbed by that heartless vixen and her hands mercilessly pounded on the bottom of his seat.

I was a woman transfixed. I had to put a stop to it. I knew I must do something to get my children out of the hands of that dreadful creature. For a few seconds I sat in my car wondering what to do. All I could see were images of that smiling, smirking face from Snobby U laughing at me, rejoicing in my suffering, and torturing my helpless children. In an instance it was over. My car, as if guided by a mind of its own, headed straight for that plastic face. I was not even aware that my hand had started the car or that my foot had touched the pedal.

I woke up with tubes everywhere and my hands chained to the bed. Two scowling uniformed men and a dozen FBI agents sat nearby waiting to take my statement and rudely read me my rights. I had no clue what was going on. Why was everyone so angry with me? Why was everyone saying that I was going to be tried for murder? Murder of whom? What children, I was still single and had no plans to marry until well after college. I know that my roommate was impossible but why would I kill a girl just because she was insensitive, spoiled, prejudiced, and the wiriest wisp of annoyance yet to be seen. All I knew was that I was going to be late for my exam. And it would not do to miss the first exam of my junior year. The master program that I was hoping to get into would certainly frown on that. I was in shock, too horrified to remember the cruelty of the last year.

When I was recovered enough, they took me to jail. Put me on trial. Said I willfully and maliciously did murder my children to keep them out of the hands of poor defenseless Jason. It did not matter that the psychologist said that I was in such an emotional state of shock that much of our old life together was still just a dream. He was confident that at the time of the accident I was far from sane. In front of everyone Jason made an impassioned speech saying that yes, I was a mad woman, a mad woman bent on absolute, unyielding control. Seeking only to amass a self-serving fortune, making me capable of supreme inhumanity like the

Medea of old. He turned to me with evil in his eyes as he said, "Even if it was an accident as she claimed, she still killed those children just as truly as if she shot them, the very day she stepped behind the wheel drunk."

Drunk I now laugh to myself. Sure, I was drunk, drunk with rage. Drunk with the heartache of any parent robbed of their home and their young. They believed him though, even though the toxicology reports showed that I was sober. Which made sense seeing that I had never tasted alcohol in my life. But that just boosted the prosecutor's claim that it was cold hard malice and premeditated murder.

Now here I am. Convicted of stealing my own company, of using fraud to sell it, of tax evasion, of murdering the senator's dear sweet daughter. But the worst of all, I am labeled a child killer. The murder of my innocent babies in an attempt to cut the throat of the pure hearted Jason, the kind knight who was rescuing them from a den of iniquity. And soon I shall die. Die for a crime I never committed. A crime that still seems more like a bad dream although each day I remember more and more.

I am ready to die. For what do I have to live anymore? All I had of value is gone. My will to live lays somewhere in a cold grave that I shall never see. The beating of my heart is as cold as the hands that called out to me that day. If I killed them, it was only in the blindness of two eyes grown dark searching and searching, a heart grown weak waiting to hear the voices of those I shall hear no more. Yes, you too may feel that I murdered my children. You too may blame me for allowing my mind to work itself up to such an uncontrolled furry that I would lose all contact with reality, that I would react with such primordial rage. And perhaps if I did not have the misfortune of living my own story, and if I had the luxury of standing safely upon an insulated bully pulpit I too would feel as you do.

They say I never should have been behind the wheel in my mental state. That my out of control car was no better than a gun waiting to go off, and that it was a sure bullet striking the heart of my determinedly stalked victim. But I know better. The real murder, the one guilty of pulling the trigger was none other than their scheming father Jason Robertson! It was he and his money grabbing new bride that killed them! It is their money loving, power hungry hands that coldly stole every fiber of my body hoping to use the children as leverage. It was their clever lawyers that found buried loopholes to void the marriage of ten years that pulled the trigger. Yes, they murdered my children! It was them, it had to be them! I could never have done it. I never could have done it! I promise! I promise! O how I promise! It was them; you just have to believe me that it was them and not I. Oh please tell me that you believe me! Please tell me that I am not the one who killed my dearest little ones! Oh, please tell me that I am innocent of this terrible, nightmarish crime!

ABOUT THE AUTHOR

Katherine B. Parilli stumbled upon her love of writing thanks in great part to her father who homeschooled her in the second and seventh grade. Blessed with a love of reading, but seemingly possessing no talent for writing, Katherine would virtually rewrite the book for her book report. Her Father, not content to have her rewrite the book for her reports, he insisted that she write, rewrite, and rewrite again and again until nearly in tears, she was finally able to write a few semi thoughtful sentences. It was in her first year of high school when this rigorous training suddenly blossomed into a love of writing everything from poetry and short stories, to novels and short research articles.

Poetry From the Heart: Poems of Faith, a collection of faith based poems, was her first book to be published. From time to time she contributes some of her poems to the Make Time for Happy 101 blog as well as the Make

Time for Happy You Tube channel. She also has her own You Tube Channel called Poetry From the Heart as well as writes a blog called Reflections about Life and KB Writes.

In her spare time, Katherine enjoys spending time in the garden, making puzzles, and playing with her dog Happy.

www.ingramcontent.com/pod-product-compliance
Lightning Source LLC
Chambersburg PA
CBHW020144150626
46552CB00021B/1671